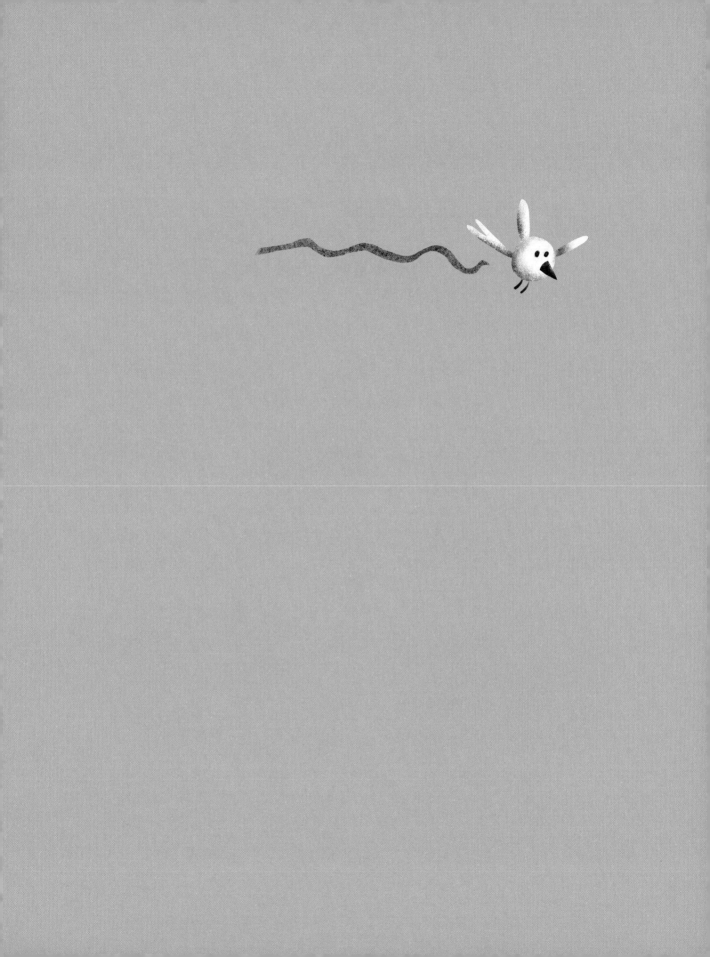

ARE

For Marrianne & Arthur

ISBN 978-0-06-286594-6

The artist used Procreate and Adobe to create the digital illustrations for this book.

Design by Coll Muir and Chelsea C. Donaldson

20 21 22 23 24   SCP   10 9 8 7 6 5 4 3 2 1

❖

First Edition

by

COLL MUIR

HARPER
An Imprint of HarperCollinsPublishers

Are you a cat?

Why do you want to know if I'm a cat?

I'm a dog, and dogs chase cats.

Well, I'm not a cat, so you can't chase me.

Okay, what are you then?

Umm . . .

I'm a bird.

You're not a bird.

Yes, I am.

Okay, if you're a bird, prove it. Fly.

Where?

Fly up to that tree.

See, you're not a bird. You are a cat.

No. I'm not a cat. I'm a . . .

squirrel.

You're not a squirrel.

Yes, I am.

Okay, if you're a squirrel,
open this nut.

Why?

Because that's what
squirrels do.

I knew that. No problem.

OUCH!

See, you're not a squirrel.
You are a cat.

No. I'm not a cat. I'm a . . .

butterfly.

You're not a butterfly.

Yes, I am.

Okay, if you're a butterfly, land on that flower without squashing it.

Why?

Because that's what butterflies do.

I knew that. Okay, watch this.

Oops.

See, you're not a butterfly. You are a cat.

No. I'm not a cat. I'm a . . .
rabbit.

You're not a rabbit.

Yes, I am.

Okay, if you're a rabbit, hop down that hole.

Why?

Because that's what rabbits do.

I knew that. Okay, watch me.

Uh-oh, I'm stuck.

I knew you're not a rabbit.

**Who cares? Please help
me out of here.**

Look, a mouse!

Do you want to chase it?

Yes, I do want to chase it.

I knew it. YOU ARE A CAT!

Yes. I am a cat.

Okay, Cat, let's chase the mouse together.

"Eek!" said
the mouse.

Stop! You can't chase me.

Oh?

Hmm . . . He's a dog and I'm a cat.
Surely, we can chase you.